Upping sticks

by Jayne Garner

Acknowledgements

Actors: Stephenson Ardern-Sodje and Rachel Barton

Copyright © Axis Education 2008

First published in Great Britain by Axis Education Ltd

ISBN 978-1-84618-128-3

Axis Education
PO Box 459
Shrewsbury
SY4 4WZ

Email: enquiries@axiseducation.co.uk

www.axiseducation.co.uk

Tom likes Kim a lot. He asks her if she wants to live with him.

She says yes! Where shall we live?

Shall we live in Tom's bedsit?

No, Kim says Tom's bedsit is too little.

Shall we live at Kim's house?

No, Tom wants to live with Kim, not her mum and dad.

Shall we live in the town centre?

No, Kim does not want to live next to Tom's friends.

Shall we live in a village?

No, Tom says there is not much to do in a village.

Shall we live in a flat?

No, Tom does not like going in lifts.

Tom says they could think about moving town.

That is not what Kim had in mind. She
would miss her mum and dad.

We could move to Liverpool, that is not too far.

Kim says she would have to get a new job if they move to Liverpool.

Shall we move to London? We could both get new jobs.

Yes, Kim says. There are lots of jobs in London.

Tom says there are lots of things to do in London too.

They think hard. Where shall we live?

Maybe a change would be good.

Let's move to London.